Art ©1999 by bohem press
Text ©2000 by Carol Diggory Shields
Cover design by Todd Sutherland
All rights reserved
CIP Data is available

Published in the United States by Handprint Books, Inc.
413 Sixth Avenue, Brooklyn, New York 11215
www.handprintbooks.com

Originally published in Switzerland
by bohem press, Zurich

First edition
Printed in China
ISBN: 1-929766-05-X
10 9 8 7 6 5 4 3 2 1

Music

paintings by
svjetlan junaković

poems by
carol diggory shields

ANIMAGICALS

HANDPRINT BOOKS

I plod through the desert
ba-rumpity-bump.
My drums keeping time,
ka-thumpity-thump.
Bumpity, thumpity,
rumpity, thump,
I am a...

From
rock
to rock
I hop and skip,
My little feet go
trip-trop-trip.
At the top
I sound my note.
Ta-dah!

camel,
with a drum
on each hump.

Down in the swamp,
when the moon
shines bright,
Hear my song,
in soft summer nights.
Swirling, skirling,
through the bog,
I'm a...

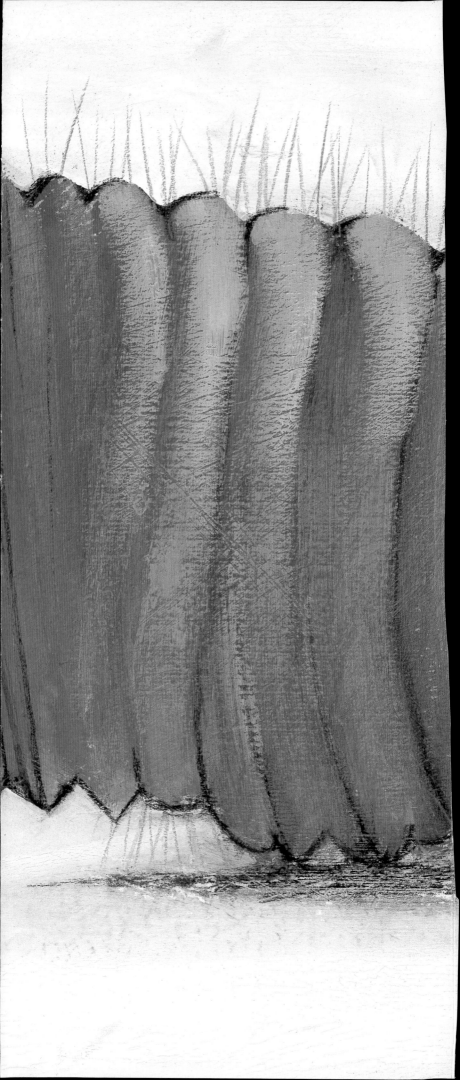

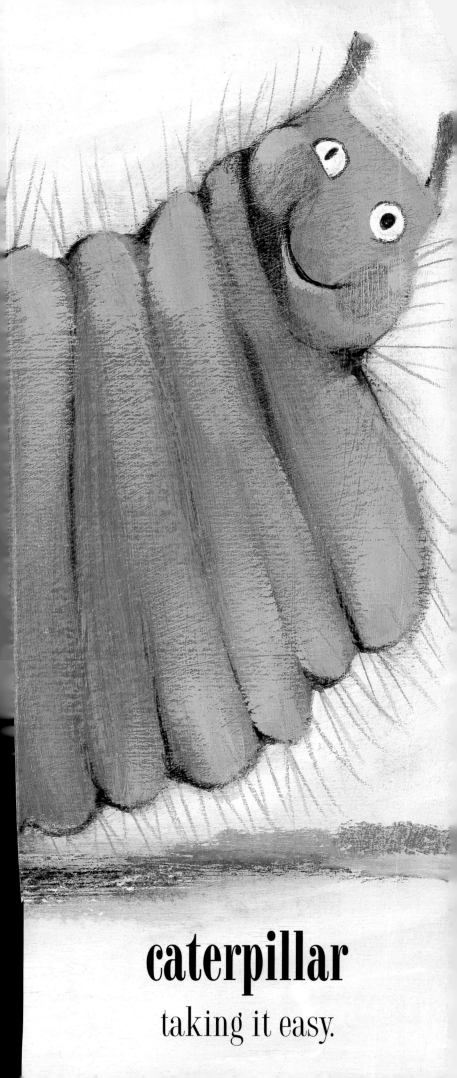

caterpillar

taking it easy.

I'm on my way
just inching along,
I'm not very
fast,

I'm
not
very
strong.

My music is squeezy and
sometimes it's wheezy,
I'm just a...

For I'm a
**mountain
goat.**

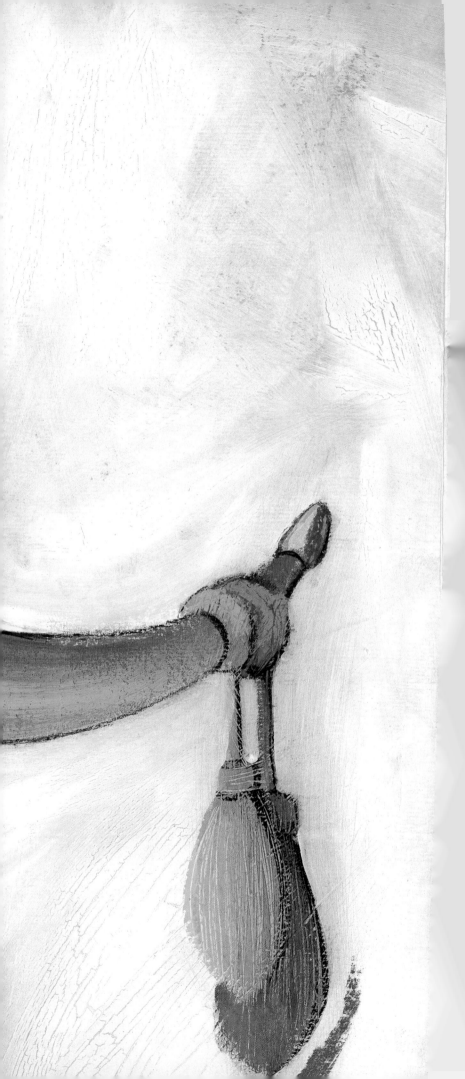

I'm a big fellow,
    I love to play cello.
The sound
    that it makes
Is so sweet
    and mellow.
      I can play music,
      'most anywhere
      For I am...

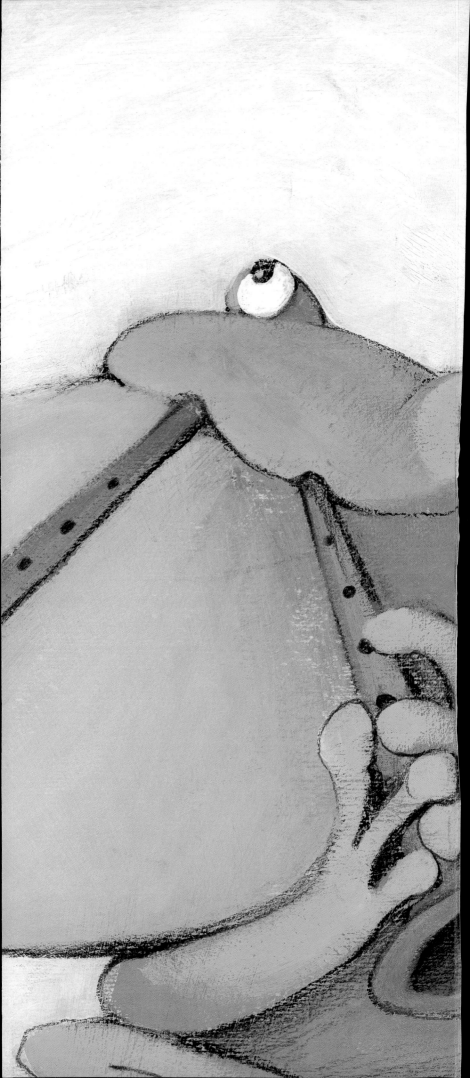

bagpipe-playing **bullfrog**.

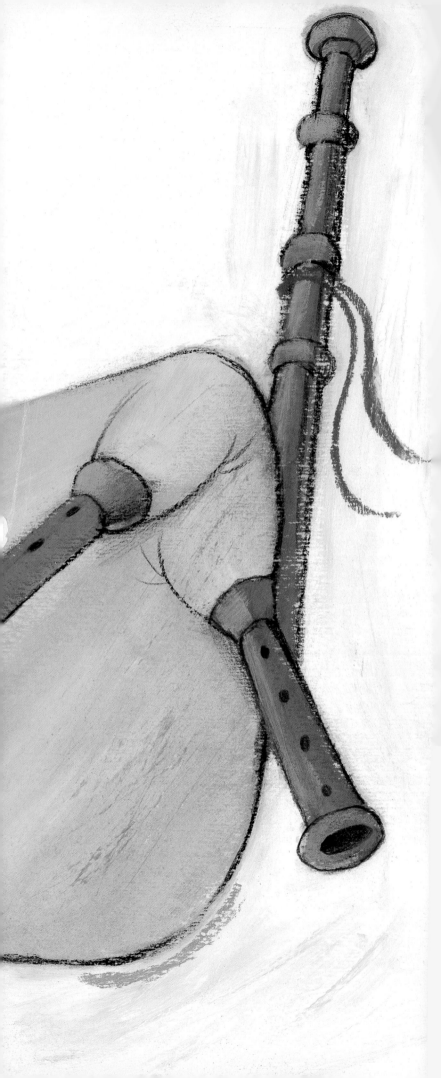

Two hands, four hands,
six hands, ten!
Up the scale
and down again.
Allegro con brio?
Watch
my speed!
It's easy
for me...

a cello who's also a
bear.

I'm a
centipede.

I'm weaving
a tune
that goes up
and down,
Back and forth
and round
and round.
The notes of
my harp
will string
you along.
I'm a...

Flute notes float up
from the blue.
With all my arms
I play for you
A lullaby
to help you sleep,
From an...

spider
spinning
a spider's
song.

My saxophone gleams
in golden curves,
I'm playing a song
that swings
and swerves.
My song is long
and so am I,

octopus
down in

the deep.

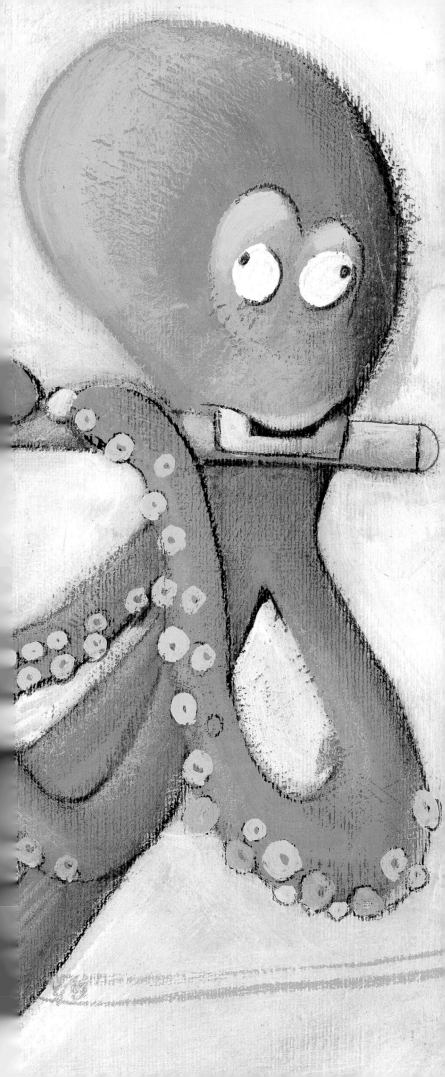

Sometimes I'm green,
sometimes I'm brown,
I have a French horn
that circles around.

I change my tune,
my colors too,

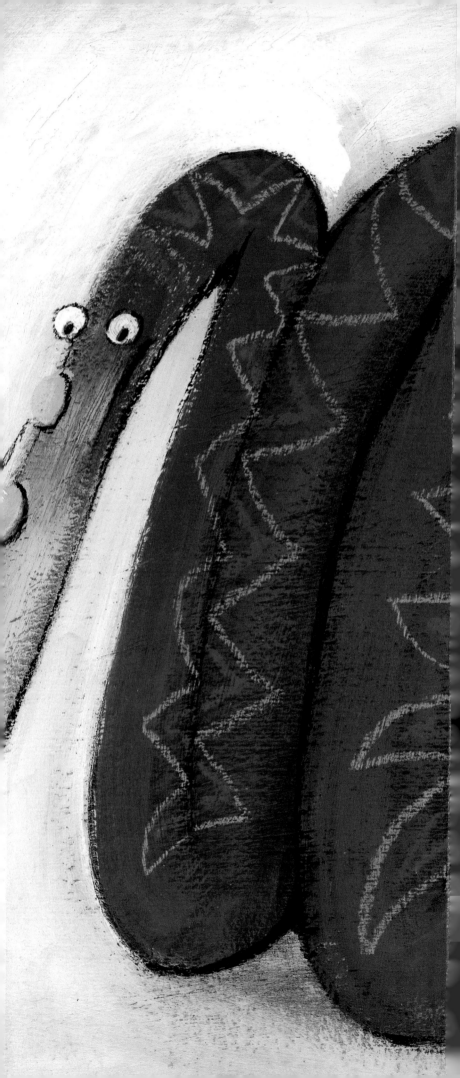

A
saxophone
snake
slithering by.

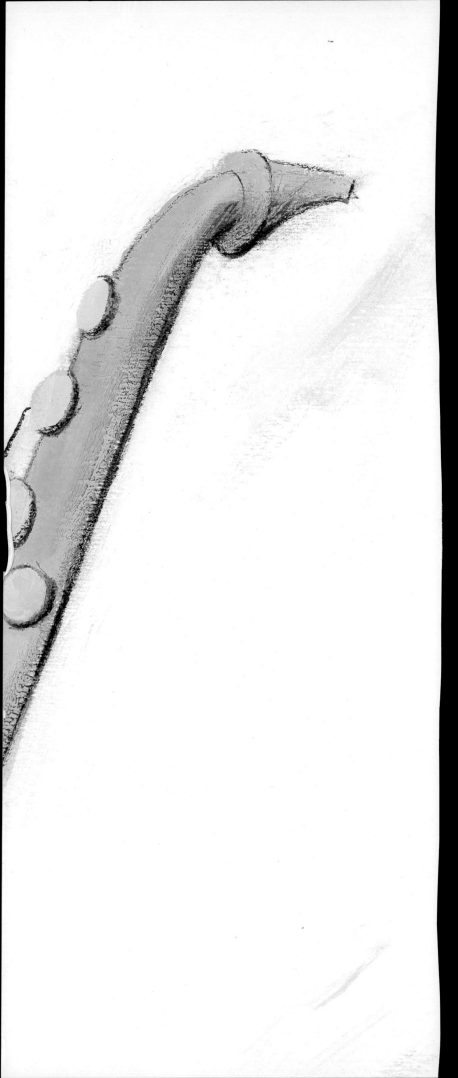

Doodling, noodling,
fast or slow,
I bring my song
wherever I go,
Hear me once
and you'll never forget...

I'm a
chameleon—
that's what
I do!

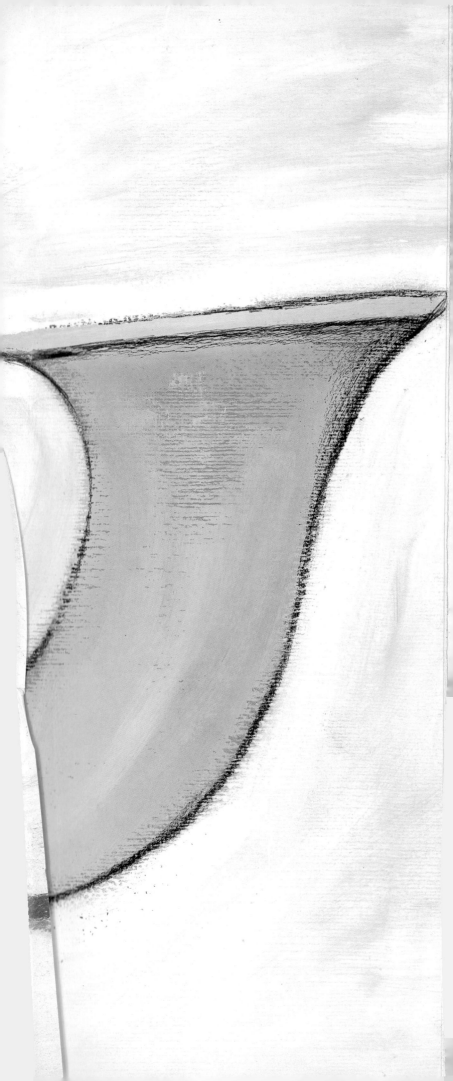

I'm the one
who keeps the beat.
I swing my tail
and stamp my feet.
Thumping on
my great big drum,
Thumping on...

This
elephant
playing on
her clarinet.

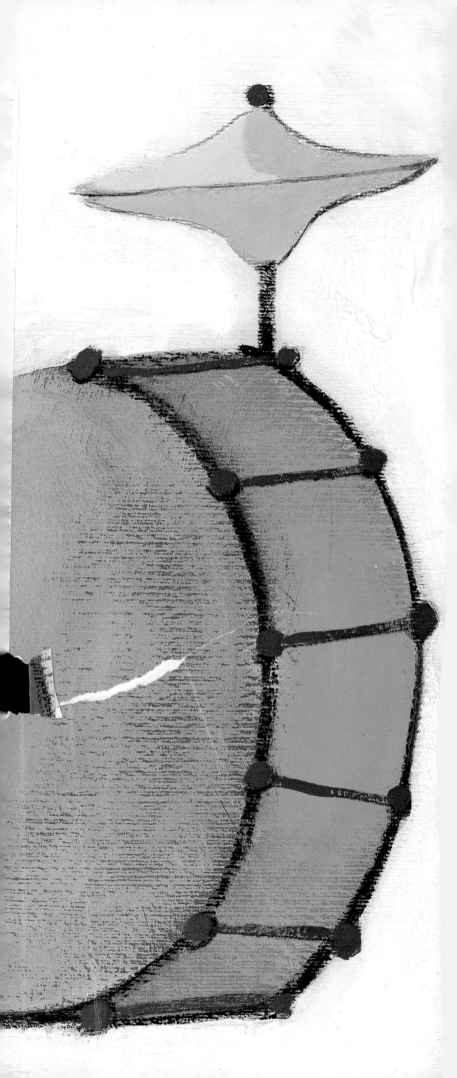

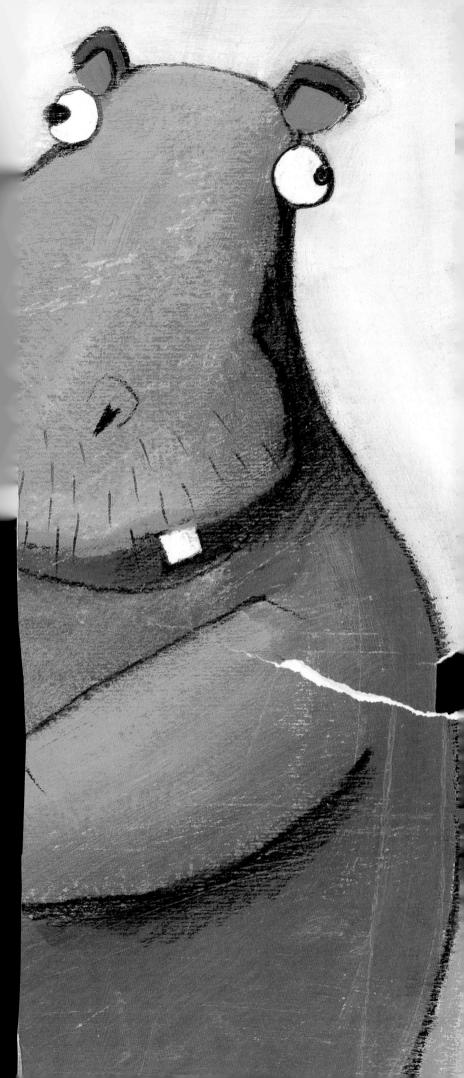

my
hippo
tum!